W9-DJP-100

DISCARDED

FOOTBALL

by Jonatha A. Brown

Reading consultant: Susan Nations, M.Ed., author/literacy coach/consultant

Please visit our web site at: www.earlyliteracy.cc
For a free color catalog describing Weekly Reader® Early Learning Library's list
of high-quality books, call 1-877-445-5824 (USA) or 1-800-387-3178 (Canada).
Weekly Reader® Early Learning Library's fax: (414) 336-0164.

Library of Congress Cataloging-in-Publication Data

Brown, Jonatha A.
    Football / Jonatha A. Brown.
      p. cm. — (My favorite sport)
    Includes bibliographical references and index.
    ISBN 0-8368-4339-8 (lib. bdg.)
    ISBN 0-8368-4346-0 (softcover)
    1. Football—Juvenile literature. I. Title.
  GV950.7.B77   2004
  796.332—dc22   2004041973

This edition first published in 2005 by
Weekly Reader® Early Learning Library
330 West Olive Street, Suite 100
Milwaukee, WI 53212 USA

Copyright © 2005 by Weekly Reader® Early Learning Library

Editor: JoAnn Early Macken
Art direction, cover and layout design: Tammy West
Photo research: Diane Laska-Swanke

Photo credits: Cover, title, pp. 15, 18, Gregg Andersen; p. 5 © Nick Laham/Getty Images; p. 7
Tammy West/© Weekly Reader Early Learning Library, 2005; p. 8 © Allen Kee/WireImage.com;
p. 9 © Tom Hauck/WireImage.com; p. 10 © Brian Bahr/Getty Images; pp. 11, 20 © Steve Grayson/
WireImage.com; p. 12 © Chris Pizzello/WireImage.com; p. 13 © Jeff Gross/Getty Images; p. 16
© Tom Pidgeon/Getty Images; p. 17 © Doug Pensinger/Getty Images; p. 21 © Kent Smith/
WireImage.com

Printed in the United States of America

1 2 3 4 5 6 7 8 9 08 07 06 05 04

Table of Contents

CHAPTER 1

Football Then and Now

Football has its roots in two British games — soccer and rugby. It came from those games in the mid-1800s. Before long, football had its own rules. But only colleges had football teams. And only men played.

The British game of rugby turned into American football. This picture shows a Rugby World Cup game.

These days, people of all ages play football. Young kids play. High schools have teams. The best college players can go on to join pro teams. There are now teams for girls and women, too. But the sport is still played mostly by boys and men.

Thousands of fans attend some college games. People flock to professional games, too. Fans near and far can watch many games on TV.

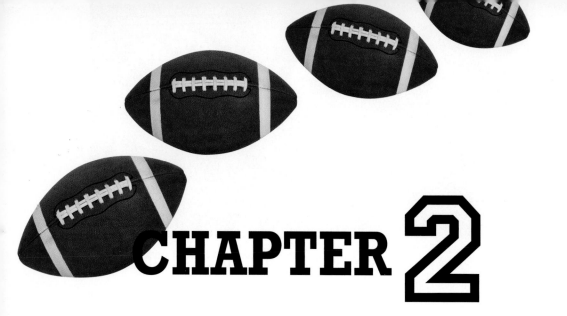

CHAPTER 2

Football Basics

Football is played on a large, long field. Yard lines cross the field every five yards. At each end of the field is a goal line. Beyond each goal line is a set of goal posts with a crossbar between them.

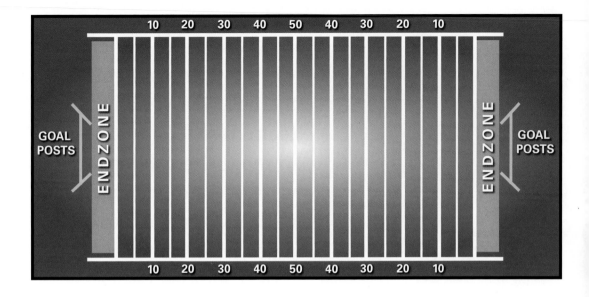

Two teams play against each other. Each team has eleven players on the field. The teams take turns trying get the football over each other's goal line. When the players on one team have the ball, the other team tries to keep them from scoring.

This is how the game works. One team gets the ball. Players on that team have four chances to move the ball ten yards toward one goal. Each chance is called a down. If the team moves the ball ten yards or more, it has made a first down. Then it gets four more downs. That means four more chances to gain at least ten more yards.

This player has moved the ball past the first-down marker.

When players do not move the football ten yards in three downs, they may punt, or kick, it to the other team on their fourth down. Then the other team gets the ball. The players try to move the ball toward the other goal.

An Oregon Ducks player blocks a punt attempt by Washington State.

A Carolina Panthers receiver celebrates after catching a touchdown pass.

There is more than one way to score. When a team runs the ball over the goal line or completes a pass over that line, it scores a touchdown. The team gets six points.

That team gets a chance to score extra points. There are two ways to do that. A player can placekick the ball over the goal line from the three-yard line. The ball must go between the goal posts and over the crossbar. If it does, the team gets one extra point.

The Oakland Raiders kick an extra point.

At the last minute, a California player dives into the end zone to score two points.

Instead of kicking an extra point, the team can try for two extra points. It can either run the ball over the goal line or pass the ball to a player who runs over the line.

Sometimes a team scores by kicking the ball across the goal line from anywhere in the field. The ball must go over the crossbar and between the goal posts. If it does, the team has made a field goal. It scores three points.

The team with the most points at the end of the game wins.

The New England Patriots win the Super Bowl with a field goal!

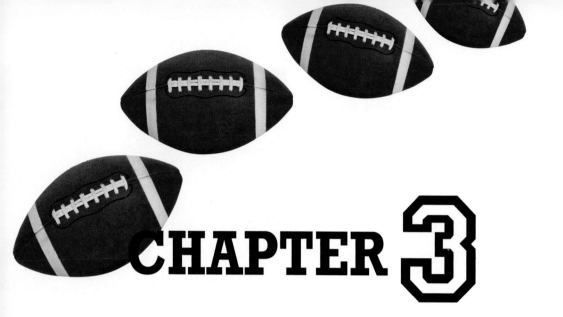

CHAPTER 3

Exciting Plays

A good football game has many exciting moments. One is a long running play. That is when a player runs the ball most of the way down the field. He dodges and slips away from players who try to tackle him. If the other team does not tackle him, he scores a touchdown.

Another great play is the long pass play. A receiver runs downfield. He tries to get in position to catch the ball. The quarterback throws the pass. If the receiver catches the ball, the pass is complete. The team gets closer to the end zone. It may even make a touchdown!

The quarterback drops back and looks for a receiver.

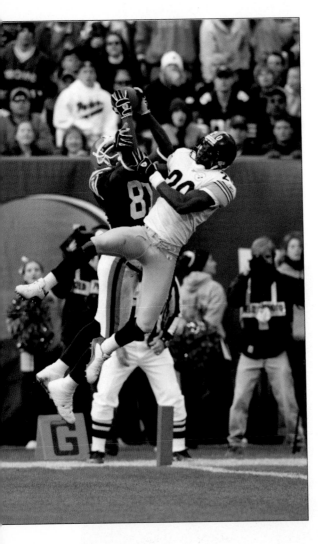

But long passes do not always work. Once the ball is in the air, anyone can catch it. If a player on the other team catches the ball, that team takes possession. The team with the ball heads for the other goal line. That team has a chance to score.

Two players fight for possession of a pass.

When a player drops the ball, we say he has fumbled. A fumble can also turn a game around. If a player on the other team recovers the fumble, that team takes possession of the ball. It is their turn to try to score.

Where is the ball? Players from both teams try to find it.

Every player on a team has an important job.

When the score is close, the end of a football game can be very exciting. Each team tries to trick the other. Both teams try to make plays that no one expects. They often make plays that surprise the fans and the other team. Almost anything can happen in the last few seconds of a close game!

CHAPTER 4

Championship Games

After the regular season ends, the playoffs begin. The top teams play each other. After a few playoff games, only two teams are left. They play one game. In that game, they fight for the championship.

A Michigan player tackles a California player during a Rose Bowl game.

In football, the championship games are called bowls. Each group of colleges has a bowl game. Some of the best college teams in the country play in the Orange Bowl. The Rose Bowl is also famous. The college bowls draw huge crowds.

The most famous football game of the year is the Super Bowl. The two best National Football League (NFL) teams play. Thousands of fans turn out to watch. Millions view the game on TV. In the United States, the Super Bowl is often the most watched sporting event of the year.

A Carolina player blocks a New England field goal attempt during the Super Bowl.

Glossary

bowls – championship games

placekick – to kick toward the goal in order to score

playoffs – games that take place after the regular season ends. A playoff decides which team will be champion.

pro (short for professional) – played as a paid job

quarterback – leader of the players whose main job is to score

receiver – player who tries to catch a forward pass in order to move the ball down the field

tackle – to grab and throw down or stop

For More Information

Books

Football. Ray Broekel (Children's Press)

Football: The Rules of the Game. Jennifer M. Sakurai (Price Stern Sloan)

The Illustrated Rules of Football. R. L. Patey (Ideals Children's Books)

Super Bowl! NFL Reader. Tim Polzer (DK Publishing)

Whiz Kid Quarterbacks NFL Reader. Tom Barnidge (DK Publishing)

Web Sites

Green Bay Packers Kids' Zone
www.packers.com/fans/KidsZone/
Football puzzles, polls, and games

Play Football
www.playfootball.com/
Football facts, news, online games, and more from the NFL

Index

About the Author

Jonatha A. Brown has been writing children's books since leaving a corporate position in 2001. She holds a B.A. in English from St. Lawrence University in Canton, New York. Jonny lives in Phoenix, Arizona, where she is a fan of the Arizona Diamondbacks. Her favorite sport is dressage.